Published by Roaring Brook Press

Roaring Brook Press is a division of Holtzbrinck Publishing Holdings Limited Partnership

120 Broadway, New York, NY 10271 • mackids.com

Our books may be purchased in bulk for promotional, educational, or business use.

Please contact your local bookseller or the Macmillan Corporate and Premium Sales Department at

(800) 221-7945 ext. 5442 or by email at MacmillanSpecialMarkets@macmillan.com.

Library of Congress Cataloging-in-Publication Data is available.

First edition, 2022

This book was edited by Emily Feinberg, designed by Mike Burroughs,

and art directed by Neil Swaab. The production editor was Taylor Pitts, and

the production manager was John Nora.

The illustrations for this book were drawn in pencil and colored digitally.

The font used throughout this book is Adobe Jenson Pro.

Printed in China by Hung Hing Off-set Printing Co. Ltd., Heshan City, Guangdong Province

ISBN 978-1-250-79698-1 (hardcover)

1 3 5 7 9 10 8 6 4 2

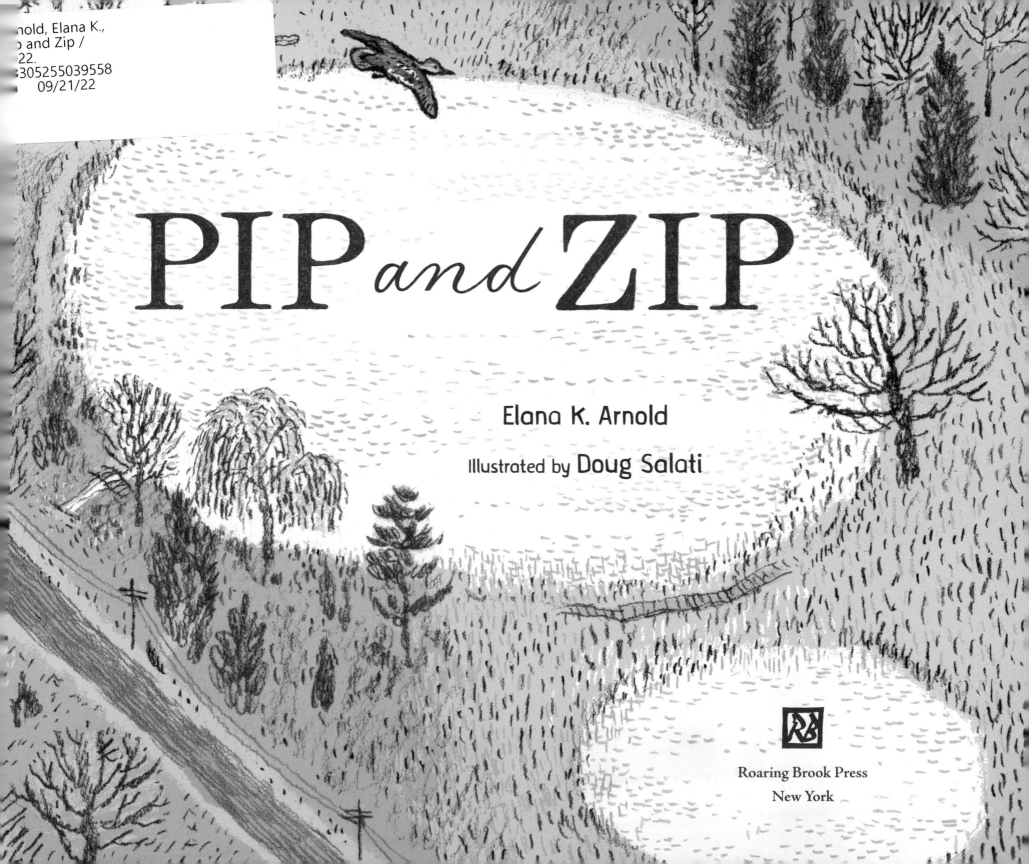

PIP and ZIP

Elana K. Arnold

Illustrated by Doug Salati

Roaring Brook Press

New York

Once, when we all had to stay home for the whole long springtime,
when schools were closed
and work was closed
and everything fun was canceled,

after we were all so bored of TV
and computers
and video games
and screens of every kind,
Dad said, "Let's take a walk."

We saw our neighbor Ted painting the trim of his windows

and the Garcia sisters roller-skating toward the school's big empty parking lot
and a kid we didn't know shooting hoops in his driveway.

At the park

people kept their dogs from sniffing one another,

which seemed to make them sad,

and the restaurant we used to go to for Saturday morning pancakes

had all its windows dark

like sleeping eyes.

We walked around the lake
bored and slow

and then—there!—what was that?

In the shallows of the water?

Dad got a stick and fished it out.

An egg!

"What's an egg doing in the water?"

"We can't just leave it here!"

So Mom put it in her pocket and on we walked.

But then . . . there!

Another egg. All by itself, half in the mud.

Mom cleaned it off and put it in her other pocket.

On the way home, we asked so many questions.

How did eggs end up in the water and the mud?

Who laid them?

Could they hatch?

We knew who we could ask.

Back on our street, Mom told Ted what we'd found
and he said, "Sometimes ducks don't know what to do
with the first eggs they lay
so they drift to the bottom of the lake
and that's that."

He said that if things weren't so topsy-turvy upside down
we would take the eggs to the wildlife center
where experts could take good care of them.

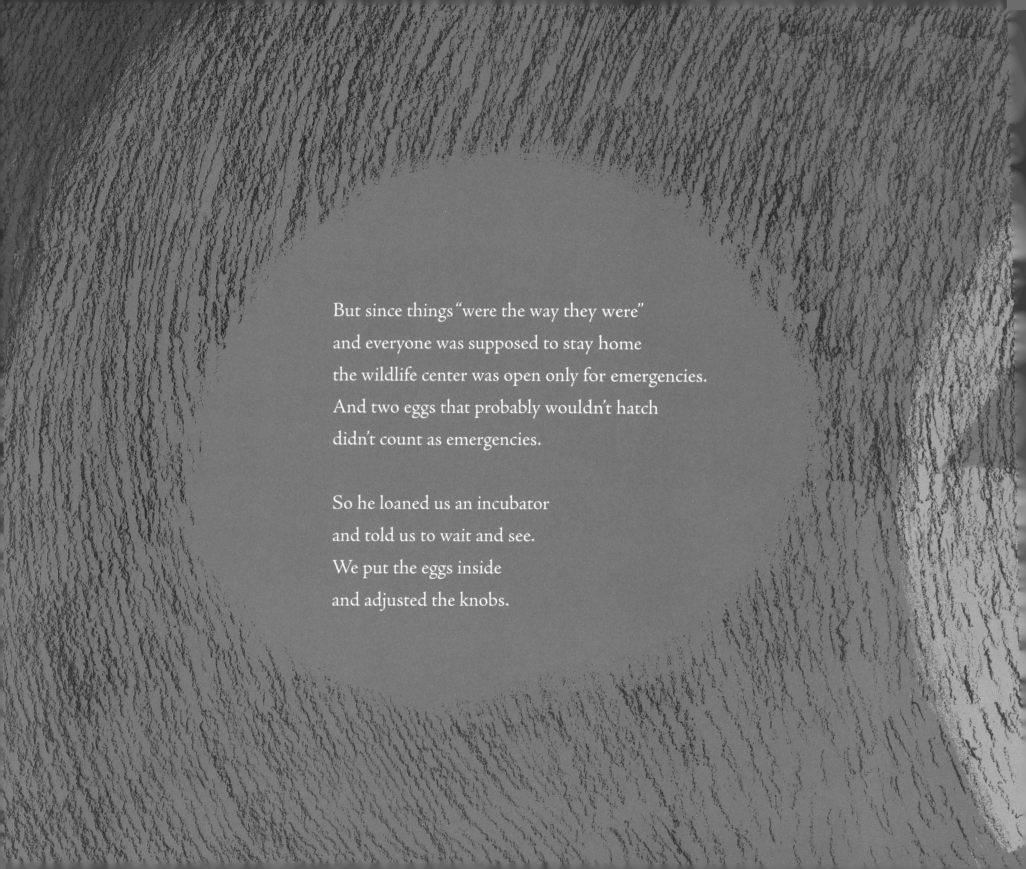

But since things "were the way they were"
and everyone was supposed to stay home
the wildlife center was open only for emergencies.
And two eggs that probably wouldn't hatch
didn't count as emergencies.

So he loaned us an incubator
and told us to wait and see.
We put the eggs inside
and adjusted the knobs.

We waited   and waited   and waited

for twenty-eight days.

That's a long time to wait.

all across the neighborhood
all around the world . . .

But everyone was waiting

anyway

the whole planet waited
with us.

And nothing happened,
nothing changed.

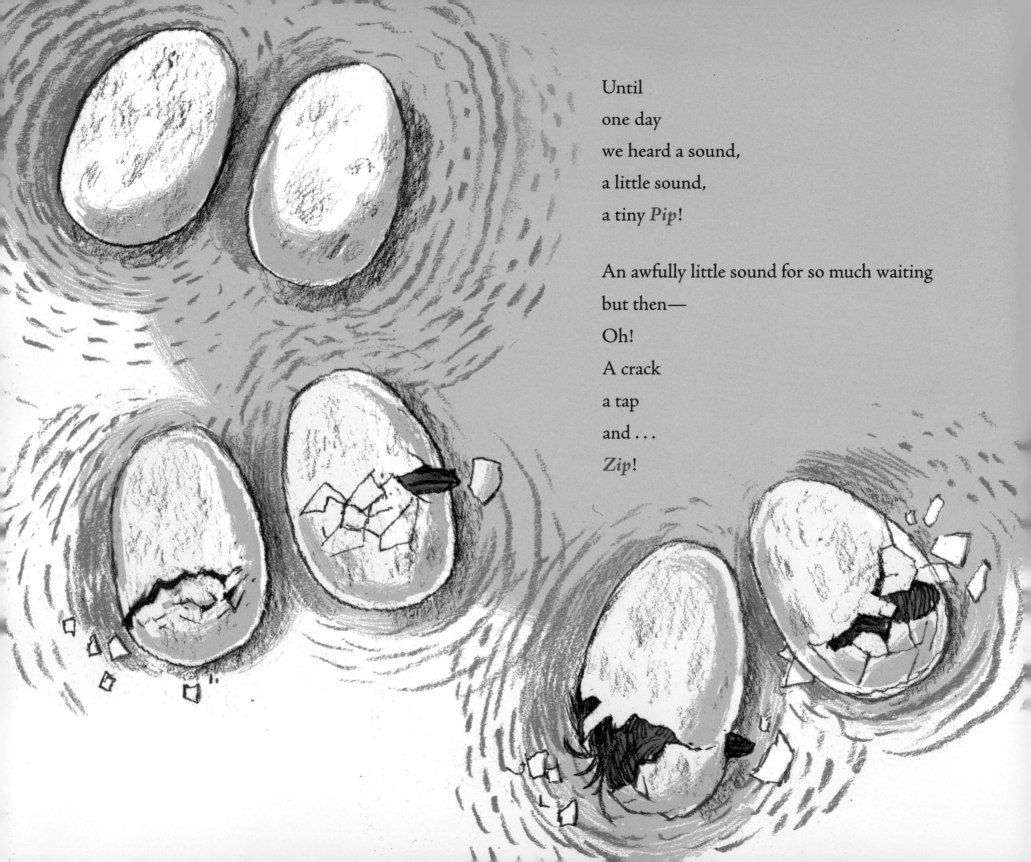

Until
one day
we heard a sound,
a little sound,
a tiny *Pip*!

An awfully little sound for so much waiting
but then—
Oh!
A crack
a tap
and . . .
Zip!

Out they came
one and then the other—
Pip
and
Zip.

Wet and small and sort of strange.
Weird floppy webbed feet they didn't know how to use.

When Ted saw what we had hatched
boy was he surprised.

"In all my years working with birds,
this is a first," he said.

Then
together,
we waited more,

and they fluffed up
and learned how to waddle

and how to sip water
and how to eat food

and how to poop
and how to swim
and how to cuddle.

And more days passed,
more home days

until
one day

Pip and Zip learned what wings are for.

And away they went
off into the great big world.

We waved goodbye
and laughed
and cried
and hugged each other tight
and wished them well.

And then
at last
we went out, too,

to tell our neighbors about **Pip** and **Zip**
to roller-skate with the Garcia sisters
to meet that kid with the basketball hoop.
Out we went, into the great blue world.

A Note from the Author

The story you just read is based on a real-life adventure my family and I had when we found two duck eggs at a pond near our home during the 2020 Covid-19 Safer at Home orders.

In normal times, under normal circumstances, we would have taken the eggs to a wildlife shelter, but we were all under strict orders to shelter in place.

You might be wondering if it's really possible for a duck egg that has sunk to the bottom of a pond to hatch. The answer is, yes! If the eggs have not yet begun to be warmed by the mama duck—if she, like the mother duck in this story, was "surprised" by early eggs—and if they are relocated to a suitable environment and incubated, there is about a 50 percent chance the eggs will hatch after a twenty-eight-day gestation period.

We were very, very lucky! Both of our eggs hatched.

The hatching process is interesting, too. First comes the "pip"—that's when the duckling makes the first crack in the shell. After even more waiting—up to three days—the duckling will "zip"—that's when it cracks the shell all the way around, splitting it in two, and emerging, at last.

We named our ducklings Pip and Zip, after the egg-hatching process. In real life, they went to our local wildlife shelter shortly after hatching, and they rejoined other mallard ducks at our local pond when they were fully grown. Some liberties have been taken with this story, as it has one foot in real life and one foot in fiction. In this book, the family that finds the eggs is fortunate that Ted, a certified wildlife rehabilitator, lives next door. He is able to assist with care for the eggs and, later, the ducklings.

The Covid-19 crisis was an unprecedented, scary, topsy-turvy time. But even in the midst of everything, there are always opportunities for joy, and love, and family.

What Should You Do If You Find a Duck Egg?

If you find unattended eggs or wild animals who look like they may need your help, please contact your local wildlife rescue agency. Though all of us want to help animals, wildlife rehabilitators are trained and licensed to do this work.

In the United States, all migratory birds—including mallards like Pip and Zip—are protected by the Migratory Bird Treaty Act, which protects birds, their feathers, their eggs, and their nests. Disturbing birds and eggs—even with good intentions—is prohibited under this Act.

If you'd like to learn more about wild birds near you and how you can help, visit audubon.org.

Visit the National Audubon Society's website for some suggestions on how to get started . . . and, even easier, just go outside and look around! The world is full of interesting birds.

A great way to get to know the birds in your local environment—whether you live in the city, the country, or the suburbs—is to be a bird watcher. Bird watching is for *everyone*.

Visit the links below for more information

National Audubon Society
audubon.org/news/easy-ways-get-kids-birding

All About Birds: Mallards
allaboutbirds.org/guide/Mallard/lifehistory#

U.S. Fish & Wildlife Service
fws.gov/birds/index.php
fws.gov/birds/policies-and-regulations/laws-legislations/migratory-bird-treaty-act.php

National Wildlife Rehabilitators Association
nwrawildlife.org/page/Found_Injured_Wildlife

The Migratory Bird Treaty Act
fws.gov/birds/policies-and-regulations/laws-legislations/migratory-bird-treaty-act.php